SO-AAG-185

# What grown-ups are saying about ClubZone kids

"In today's world, where our children are inundated by negative and amoral messages, the ClubZone Kids books infuse positive, Christian thoughts into the next generation. I highly recommend these books with enthusiasm."

—Pediatric neurosurgeon Benjamin S. Carson, best-selling author of *Gifted Hands* and the focus of a Today's Heroes series book

"In ClubZone Kids, Joel Thompson brings godly principals to life for children, and he wraps biblical truths into warm human stories that youngsters can relate to."

—Bill Myers, best-selling author of *The Incredible Worlds of Wally McDoogle* and *McGee and Me*

"Joel Thompson takes real life stories and tells how things just sometimes go bad. The biblical truth of the stories is given in a manner that will hold the attention of his readers while unfolding in a clear way godly principles. The stories also do an excellent job of dealing with the realities of interpersonal relationships of children."

—Ken Smitherman, president, Association of Christian Schools International

Books in the ClubZone Kids series:

# Shortcuts

## & Other Stories
## That Teach Christian Values

## Joel Thompson

Baker Books
A Division of Baker Book House Co
Grand Rapids, Michigan 49516

© 2002 by Joel Thompson

Published by Baker Books
a division of Baker Book House Company
P.O. Box 6287, Grand Rapids, MI 49516-6287

Printed in the United States of America

All rights reserved. No part of this publication may be reproduced, stored in
a retrieval system, or transmitted in any form or by any means—for example,
electronic, photocopy, recording—without the prior written permission of the
publisher. The only exception is brief quotations in printed reviews.

**Library of Congress Cataloging-in-Publication Data**

Thompson, Joel, 1952–
   Shortcuts & other stories that teach Christian values / Joel Thompson.
      p.   cm. —(ClubZone kids ; 2)
   Contents: The great garage sale : a story about giving all for God — Craig
the Complainer : a story about grumbling and praising — Nate to the res-
cue! : a story about loving a neighbor — Carlos's toothache : a story about
strength in Jesus — Roses for Natasha : a story about coveting and content-
ment — Shortcuts : a story about doing your best — The innocent thief : a
story about thinking the best — Never enough : a story about thankfulness.
   ISBN 0-8010-4510-X (pbk.)
   1. Christian life—Juvenile fiction. 2. Children's stories, American. [1.
Conduct of life—Fiction. 2. Christian life—Fiction. 3. Short stories.] I. Title
II. Title: Shortcuts and other stories that teach Christian values. III. Series:
Thompson, Joel, 1952– . ClubZone kids ; 2.
PZ7.T3715955Sh 2003
[E]—dc21                                   2002009505

Scripture quotations are taken from the HOLY BIBLE, NEW INTERNATIONAL
READER'S VERSION ®. NIrV ®. Copyright © 1995, 1996, 1998 by the International
Bible Society. Used by permission of Zondervan. All rights reserved.

For current information about all releases from Baker Book House, visit our
web site:
                       http://www.bakerbooks.com

Interior design by Brian Brunsting

Dedicated
to my sons,
Joel,
Michael,
and
David

# CLUBZONE KIDS
## Cast of Characters

**Carlos** has one big dream . . . to just "fit in!" But, as Carlos will be the first to admit, he has a lot of growing up to do.

**Danny** calls himself the King of Fun! He is a born leader! Well . . . when he wants to be.

**Heather** is not shy! Everyone knows she loves to be the center of attention. A real social butterfly, but one with a kind heart.

**Natasha** is an artistic, active little girl who sometimes doesn't think things all the way through. But, hey, she's working on it!

**Michael** is one of the most level-headed kids in the neighborhood. Everyone thinks he'll be President of the United States one day.

### . . . & others . . .
Craig, Nate, Stacy, Brian, Karen

# Contents

7

# Dear Parents

After working for more than sixteen years to impart faith in God and biblical values to young people, I've learned that Christian character begins at a parent's knee.

The ClubZone Kids series was created for this—so the virtues of Christlike character can be imparted by loving parents in fun, personal, entertaining, and lasting ways at home, church, and even school.

Each book in the series features eight short stories that follow the ClubZone Kids through adventures in their everyday lives. Especially designed for six- to eight-year-olds, books in the series can be read by you to young listeners or by the children themselves. Watch and see how your kids identify with characters in the series and actually begin to live the good values being taught!

In this volume, children will see how to

- give all for God
- stop grumbling and start praising
- love a neighbor
- find strength in Jesus
- stop coveting and find contentment
- do their best
- think well of others, and
- be thankful

So while you'll find books in the series a valuable tool for conveying important life principles in delightful, interesting ways, your children will find the stories memorable and just plain fun. The idea's simple, really, but the goal life-giving: Encourage children to develop their understanding of God's big truths and to incorporate his virtues and values into their own lives!

Your friend,

Joel Thompson

# Dear Readers

Do you know what's really awesome about life? Every day you get to make new choices! YOU get to decide how each chapter in the story of your life will turn out! Sometimes, you hit the ball right out of the park and—home run! Other times, you might fumble or, to be honest, blow it . . .

Welcome to the ClubZone!

In the ClubZone, you will meet Danny, Michael, Heather, Natasha, and Carlos, who probably do the same sorts of things you do. But you won't just meet them—you will get to live with them, go to school with them, and try their adventures too. That's when you'll see that you're not the only one with ups and downs!

So come on and join the fun. You're only a page away from entering the ClubZone!

Your friend,

Joel Thompson

# The Great Garage Sale

*A Story about Giving All for God*

Heather chewed on her pencil as she tried to figure out the last problem of her math assignment. She didn't want to do her homework, though. She wanted to play with her dolls.

Heather looked at her doll collection, which was sitting on shelves in her room. She had all sorts of dolls—more than any other girl she knew. She spent all her allowance money on them, because dolls were just about her favorite thing in the whole world.

Heather turned back to her assignment. *I've got*

*to finish my homework before I can play with my dolls*, she thought. She did the last math problem, then looked at her next assignment.

"Okay," she said to herself, "I have to search through the newspaper and find a good news story. Then I have to read it and explain it in front of the whole class tomorrow."

Heather got out the newspaper, found an interesting story, and wrote a short report about it. After she finished the assignment, she continued to flip through the newspaper, looking for the comics. As she was looking through the paper, something caught her eye—a picture of a lady with a special doll.

"That's the most beautiful doll I've ever seen!" Heather exclaimed. As she read the story, she learned that this lady made one-of-a-kind dolls. The dolls were very expensive, because no two dolls were alike. They were made especially for one person.

The story also said that this woman was coming to town to speak at a luncheon next week. The last line of the story listed a number to call for more information.

Heather ran to the phone, dialed the number, and asked for information. When she found out how much the doll cost, she couldn't believe her ears. She didn't know people had that much money to spend on dolls!

*But I've just got to have it*, she thought after she hung up the phone.

Later that night, when Mom came home from choir practice, Heather ran downstairs and said excitedly, "Mom! Mom! Look at the picture of this doll."

"Wow, that's some doll all right," Mom said as she looked at the newspaper article.

"I've got to have this, Mom, but I don't have enough money. Could you give me some?"

Mom shook her head. "I'm sorry, Heather, but I can't do that. I already give you an allowance, and I'm not giving you any more money than that. You're going to have to forget about the doll."

But Heather couldn't forget about the doll.

She couldn't get it out of her mind, no matter how hard she tried. When she went to bed, she was still thinking about it. *How am I going to get enough money to buy that doll?* she wondered as she drifted off to sleep.

The next night, Heather sat in her room, rocking back and forth in her rocking chair, thinking of how she could get some money. As she was rocking, she looked at her collection. What a great addition that special doll would make! She had so many dolls, but that doll in the article would be one of a kind. Suddenly, a thought hit her. "Wait a minute," she said to herself. "What if I . . ."

She ran to her mom. "Mom! Mom! I've got a great idea. I know how I can get that doll!"

"What are you talking about, Heather?"

She sat down next to Mom. "Is it all right if I have a garage sale this weekend?"

"A garage sale?"

"Yeah, Mom," Heather continued. "I'm going to sell all the dolls that I've been collecting."

Mom looked surprised. "Heather, those dolls

mean so much to you. I don't know if selling them is such a good idea."

"Mom, please, I've got to have that doll," Heather pleaded, looking into her mother's eyes. "I could have the biggest doll garage sale you ever saw. Can I do it, Mom, please?"

Mom took a moment to think. Then she looked at her daughter and said, "OK, Heather. The dolls belong to you and are yours to do with as you please."

So that weekend, Heather had her garage sale. She made some signs and put them all over the neighborhood. A lot of people came to the sale, and Heather sold every last one of her dolls. But when she counted her money, she knew that she still didn't have enough.

Heather felt very sad. "How am I ever going to get that doll, Mom?" she asked.

"Well, even if you don't have enough money to buy the doll, we can still go and look at it," Mom said, giving Heather a hug.

The next week, Heather and her mom went to

the hotel where the luncheon had taken place. Heather walked over to a man who stood behind the information desk.

"Excuse me," she said. "There's a lady who's speaking about one-of-a-kind dolls. Do you know where I could find her?"

The man at the front desk told her that the woman was in the convention room down the hall. So Heather and her mom walked to the convention room. There was nobody there except for a few people cleaning up.

Heather walked over to a woman who was packing up some things in a case. "Excuse me," she said. "There was a lady here who spoke about one-of-a-kind dolls."

"That's right," the woman replied as she turned around.

Heather couldn't believe her eyes. "It's you! You're the doll lady from the newspaper," she gasped.

Heather then told the lady about how she had a big doll collection but had sold it to buy this one-of-a-kind doll. After she had poured out her heart, Heather asked, "Can I buy the doll in the paper, please? I've just got to have it."

"You realize," the woman said, "that the doll costs more than you have."

"Yes, I know," Heather said, "but I sold everything for that doll."

The woman smiled and reached for a funny-shaped briefcase. She opened it up.

"Wow!" Heather exclaimed. "That's the doll in the picture!" As she moved closer, she said, "Oh, she's even more beautiful than in the picture!"

And then Heather's dream came true. The woman said, "She's yours for the money you have."

Heather was so happy! She gratefully gave the woman the money, then left the hotel with Mom, carrying the beautiful doll in her arms. Then Mom put her hand on Heather's shoulder.

"You know, Heather," she said, "we can learn something from the way you got this doll. When we are Christians, we must be willing to give up everything to follow God. Just like you gave up all your dolls for this one special doll, we must give up everything we have for God."

Heather looked at her new doll and smiled. "It's worth it, though, isn't it, Mom?"

Mom smiled back. "It sure is, Heather."

---

*I consider everything to be nothing compared to knowing Christ Jesus. . . . Because of him I have lost everything. But I consider all of it to be garbage so I can get to know Christ.*
Philippians 3:8

# Craig the Complainer

*A Story about Grumbling and Praising*

Danny was sitting alone, reading a book at the Boys Club, a place in the neighborhood where boys could get together and play. As he was reading, he noticed a boy staring out the window. Danny knew most of the boys who belonged to the Boys Club. He decided this kid must be a new member, so he went to introduce himself.

"Hi! My name is Danny. What's your name?"

"My name's Craig," the boy replied.

"I've never seen you here before," Danny said in a friendly manner. "Are you new in town?"

"No, I've lived here for a while, but I just joined the Boys Club today," Craig said, continuing to look out the window.

"Well, how about I give you a tour of the club?" Danny said. Craig nodded his head.

First, Danny took Craig upstairs and showed him the gymnasium. Some kids were doing gymnastics, while others played basketball.

"It's too noisy in here for me," Craig shouted.

So Danny took him downstairs and showed him the swimming pool. Some kids were swimming laps, while others dove off the diving boards.

"It's so hot in here," Craig whined. "Why do they have it so hot?"

"I guess it's so no one will catch cold," Danny said as they stood looking down at the boys in the pool.

"Yeah, but this heat is steaming up my glasses," Craig continued. "They're foggy. I can't see."

So Danny took Craig down to the basement, where there was a large game room. Some kids were playing ping pong, while others played video games.

"There are too many people in here. How can you stand to be in a room with so many people?" Craig asked Danny.

"I don't know. I guess I never thought about it," Danny replied. "I just have fun."

"Well, I can't stay here," Craig said, heading for the door. "It's too crowded for me."

Danny stood there for a moment, wondering what was the matter with Craig. But he decided he wanted to be Craig's friend, so he followed him out of the game room.

"Hey! What's the matter?" Danny asked.

"I just don't like crowds. That's all," Craig grumbled.

Next, Danny took Craig to the snack shop, because he was feeling a bit hungry.

"I'll have some french fries and a sandwich, please," Danny said to the person behind the counter.

When it was Craig's turn to order, he stood there

for a while, looking at the menu sign. "Well, nothing here looks good to me. I guess I'll just have what Danny's having."

While they were eating their sandwiches, Danny decided to get to know Craig a little better. "What made you join the Boys Club now, since you've lived here for so long?" he asked.

"My mom made me join," Craig answered. "She said she didn't want me around the house complaining anymore. She told me to go out and have fun."

"Well, it doesn't look like you're having much fun to me," Danny said between bites.

"I am having fun," Craig said loudly. "I just don't like noisy places, steamy glasses, crowded rooms, and people asking me questions all the time."

"OK," Danny replied. *Boy, this kid isn't going to be much fun,* he thought.

As they were finishing their sandwiches, some of Danny's friends came over and asked him to play basketball.

"Do you want to play ball with us too?" a boy asked Craig.

"No, I don't think so," Craig said, shaking his head.

So the boys went off to play without him. After that day, Craig acted unhappy every time he came to the club. He complained about everything. Soon, none of the other boys wanted to be around him.

One day, Danny had a birthday party at his house. All of his friends were there, including Craig. However, most of the boys refused to play with Craig.

"Danny," one boy said, "why did you have to invite him? He'll ruin the whole party."

"I know," Danny said. "But he's my friend. Let's just try to have fun anyway."

So the boys began playing a game of pin-the-tail-on-the-donkey. But Craig didn't join in. Danny felt bad about this, so he went to talk to his mom.

"Mom," he said, "nobody likes playing with

Craig because he complains all the time. What can I do so all the guys will like him more?"

Mom ruffled Danny's hair. "How about we go have a talk with him?" she said.

The two of them walked over to where Craig was sitting, watching the other boys play.

"You don't seem to be having a very good time, Craig," Mom said. "What's the matter?"

"Nothing," he replied.

"Well, I hear no one wants to play with you because you're always complaining. Is that true?"

"No. I don't think I complain too much," he said. "My mom says I'm always complaining, my dad says I'm always complaining, and my sisters say I'm always complaining, but I think they're wrong. As a matter of fact, I wish they would stop saying that. They always—"

"There you go," Mom said. "What you're doing right now is complaining. Do you realize that?"

"No . . ."

"Craig," she said, sitting next to him, "for some people, complaining is a bad habit. They don't even realize when they're doing it. And it's a habit that makes God very sad. God wants you to be happy, but when you complain, it means you're not satisfied. Are you satisfied?" she asked.

"Yeah," Craig said softly. "But I don't know how to be anything other than what I am."

"Then why don't we ask God to help you enjoy yourself and stop complaining?" Mom suggested.

"OK," he agreed. So Mom, Danny, and Craig closed their eyes and prayed.

After they finished praying, Danny and Craig went to join the other boys. When the guys saw Craig coming, they mumbled, "Oh no! Here comes Craig. He's going to ruin the game."

Craig overheard them. "Wait!" he said. "I'm not going to complain anymore!"

"You're not? Why?" one boy asked.

"Because it makes God unhappy, and I don't want to make him unhappy."

The boys looked at each other and shrugged their shoulders. "Maybe he won't complain anymore," another boy said.

"We'll never know unless we give him a chance," Danny encouraged.

So the boys decided to give Craig a chance. They continued playing the game—but this time, Craig joined them. And he didn't complain once!

---

*Do everything without finding fault or arguing.*
Philippians 2:14

# Wilbur to the Rescue!

*A Story about Loving a Neighbor*

Wilbur didn't want to move. He lived in the mountains, where people had their own way of talking, their own way of dressing, and their own way of thinking. Wilbur was happy living in the mountains. After all, there were plenty of tall trees to climb and lots of neat places to play.

But one day, Wilbur's dad decided that the family should move to the city. He had gotten a new job, which would give them more food to eat and nicer clothes to wear. Right now, Mom made most of their clothes by hand, and when something got a bit too small, it was passed down to the next child—and hopefully it would fit just right.

Wilbur didn't want to leave the mountains, but when he arrived in the city, he became excited. He had never lived in a big city before! He was especially excited to go to church. He wanted to meet some new Christian friends.

On Sunday, Wilbur decided he would try to fit in with the other kids. After church, he saw a group of boys his age standing around and talking. He walked over to introduce himself.

"Hi! My name is Wilbur," he said, sticking out his hand with a smile.

None of the boys shook his hand. They didn't say anything either. They just looked at him in disgust and walked away.

*I wonder if I did something wrong?* Wilbur thought. *Maybe I interrupted their conversation. That was pretty rude of me, I guess.* He looked at the boys and scratched his head.

Then Wilbur saw a group of girls on the other side of the room. "Maybe they'll talk to me," he said to himself. He patted down his hair and walked over to the girls.

"Hi, girls!" he said, sticking out his hand with a smile. "My name is Wilbur."

The girls stared at him for a moment, then turned and walked away.

"Where in the world did he get those ugly clothes?" one said, giggling.

"Yeah," another agreed, "they don't even fit right."

"His hair's too long too. Maybe someone should tell him to get a haircut!"

The girls all laughed.

Wilbur felt very bad. Every Sunday after that, no one would play with him or talk to him. Pretty soon, he didn't even want to go to church anymore. But every night he prayed to Jesus that he would make new friends.

The one thing Wilbur looked forward to was the overnight camping trip the church group was going to take. He missed being in the country! The other kids were excited about the trip too. After all, most of them had never even been to the woods.

Finally, the big day arrived. Wilbur was the first one to get on the bus. One by one, the other boys and girls came on after him. Some kids sat in front of him, some kids sat behind him, and some kids sat across the aisle from him. But no one sat beside him.

Wilbur was very sad. He had been praying every night to Jesus that he would make new friends, yet there he sat, friendless.

Tears started to roll down his cheeks as he looked out the window. He covered his face with his hands and prayed to Jesus again. "Lord, I don't understand," he prayed. "I know you love me, but you're not answering my prayers. No one likes me. I don't have any friends."

While he was crying, he remembered a song that he sang in church. "Jesus loves me, this I know. For the Bible tells me so." Wilbur hummed the song and felt a little bit better.

When they got to the camp area, everyone

got off the bus. Some sat around the campfire and sang songs, some played games, and some went for a hike through the woods. But Wilbur remained by himself with no one to talk to or play with.

At the end of the day, the group leader, Mr. Smith, blew his whistle and called for everyone to gather round. He wanted to take a roll call before supper.

"OK, gang!" he yelled. "Let's all get together. I want to count heads and make sure everyone is present and accounted for before we eat." He pulled out a list and started to call off the names. "Kara, James, Kim, Tom, Brandon," he called. He went down the list, counting as he went.

But two of the kids didn't answer when their names were called. Mr. Smith counted again. "One, two, three, four," he said aloud as he counted each head. But, sure enough, two kids were missing.

"Listen, gang," he announced, "it looks like Natasha and Michael have wandered off by themselves, so I'm going to find them. I want you kids to stay here."

So Mr. Smith and a few other adults went through the woods, calling for Natasha and Michael.

The other kids became frightened. Where were Natasha and Michael? It was getting dark. "Maybe something happened to them," one of the kids whispered.

When Mr. Smith came back, Natasha and Michael weren't with him. He counted heads again. "One, two, three, four," he counted. "Wait a minute! Now I'm missing three people!" He called off the names again, and sure enough, three kids were missing. Natasha, Michael, and Wilbur.

"Did anyone see Wilbur?" Mr. Smith asked, sounding very nervous.

The kids all shook their heads. No one knew where Wilbur had gone. Now they were really scared.

"Maybe a wild animal got them!" one little girl said.

All of a sudden, the kids heard noises off to the side of the camp area.

"Maybe it's a bear!" squeaked a boy.

"Maybe it's a mountain lion!" shrieked a girl.

But it wasn't a scary wild beast. It was Wilbur, Natasha, and Michael!

"What happened to you?" the kids screamed excitedly.

"Wilbur found us," Natasha said.

"Yeah, we were lost until Wilbur came," Michael added happily.

But Mr. Smith did not look happy. He walked up to Wilbur and said, "Why didn't you come to me first? I'm glad you found them, but you shouldn't have gone off alone. Wilbur, why did you do this?"

Very slowly, Wilbur looked up at Mr. Smith and said, "I'm sorry. I tried to tell you, but you wouldn't listen to me. Nobody would talk to me. I tried to tell everyone that I could find them. I used to live in a place like this."

Mr. Smith was quiet for a moment. Finally, he

spoke. "I'm sorry, Wilbur. I'm sorry I didn't listen to you. We're all glad you found Natasha and Michael." He gave him a hug.

Then Michael walked up to Wilbur. "Why did you come to find us? We were always so mean to you."

Wilbur smiled. "Because Jesus wants us to love other people, no matter what. Even when they're mean to us."

"But weren't you scared?" Michael asked.

"Scared of what?" he replied.

"You know, the woods, the dark, and the animals."

"Of course not," said Wilbur. "Why would I be afraid of the woods? I used to play in the woods all the time when I lived in the mountains. Once, I even saw a bear."

"Wow! You did?" another boy gasped.

"We've never known anyone who saw anything like that," a girl added.

The kids were all excited to hear more about Wilbur's adventures in the mountains. As they gathered around the campfire to roast hot dogs, he told them story after story. Before he knew it, Wilbur had more friends than he ever had in his whole life!

---

*Love your enemies. . . . Pray for those*
*who treat you badly.*
Luke 6:27–28

# Carlos's Toothache

*A Story about Strength in Jesus*

Ouch! Carlos woke up in the middle of the night. His tooth hurt! He was scared, because he'd never had a toothache before.

"Mom! Mom!" he yelled.

Carlos's mom came into his room. "What is it, Carlos?" she asked as she turned on the light.

"Mom, something's wrong," he said, holding his face with his hand. "My tooth hurts. It hurts real bad!"

Mom sat down on the bed. "In the morning,

we'll go to the dentist," she said, putting her arm around him. "He'll know just what to do."

"But I hate going to the dentist," Carlos cried. "What's he going to do to me?"

"Well, Carlos," Mom said, "he'll take a look and see what the problem is. Then he'll fix it. I'll give you some aspirin right now to help some of the pain go away. Then you need to try to get some sleep."

Carlos tried his best to get some sleep, but it was no use. Even after he took some aspirin, the tooth still hurt a little bit. And he was worried about what the dentist would do to him. But, finally, he fell asleep.

When Carlos and his mom arrived at the dentist's office the next day, Carlos took a look around. There were all kinds of people waiting in the reception area. Even some other kids.

While his mother talked with the secretary, Carlos walked over to another boy.

"My tooth really hurts a lot," Carlos said. "Does yours hurt too?"

The boy looked at him. "Nah, I'm just here for a checkup," he said. "They want to make sure I don't have any cavities. Hey, maybe you've got a cavity. Maybe they'll pull your tooth out!"

Carlos didn't like the sound of that. "Pull it out!" he said. "I've never had anybody pull a tooth out. That must hurt a lot!"

"Yep, maybe they'll pull your tooth right out," the boy said, showing his teeth. "I bet they yank it out with pliers. Ouch!"

Carlos was very scared! He didn't want to get his tooth yanked out with pliers.

A little while later, the dentist's assistant called out his name. "You're next, Carlos," she said sweetly.

Carlos didn't want to go, but his mom grabbed his hand and walked with him to the dentist's room.

"Have a seat," the dentist said in a friendly voice. "I just want to see what the problem is."

"Do I have to?" Carlos asked, looking up at his mom.

"Yes, Carlos," Mom said. "Do what the dentist says."

So Carlos got into the chair, and the dentist turned on the overhead light. "Open your mouth, Carlos. I want to see your teeth."

Carlos opened his mouth, and the doctor came closer to take a look. Then Carlos remembered the pliers. He screamed.

"No!" He jumped from the chair and ran out of the room. He ran through the waiting room and out the door.

Carlos's mom finally caught up with him outside. "Carlos, what's the matter?" she asked, trying to catch her breath.

"I don't want the dentist to look at my teeth. I don't want to get my tooth taken out!" he cried.

"Carlos," Mom said tenderly, "you didn't give him a chance."

Carlos sat down on the curb and frowned. "I'm not going back in there, Mom. He was going to poke around in my mouth. And I don't want nobody in my mouth!" he stated firmly.

Mom tried to talk Carlos into going back into the dentist's office, but he wouldn't budge. After a while, she gave up, and they went home.

But Carlos's tooth still hurt. He tried to hide the pain he was feeling, but Mom saw him holding his mouth.

"Carlos," she said, "you've got to get your tooth fixed. You're in pain."

"I don't want to go to the dentist!" Carlos grabbed the bedpost. He figured that if he held on tightly, nobody could move him.

"Carlos, you've got to get your tooth fixed. What if we ask Jesus to be with you while you're at the dentist? Why don't we say a prayer for strength? Then we'll go back and get your tooth fixed."

"OK, Mom," Carlos agreed. "Maybe if I ask Jesus to be with me, I won't be so scared."

So Carlos and Mom prayed that God would give him strength. Then they went back to the dentist's office.

"It's good to have you back," the dentist said as Carlos entered the room.

Carlos didn't say a word. He figured that as long as his mouth was shut, he was in good shape.

"OK, let's start over again. Please, have a seat, Carlos."

He sat down in the chair as the dentist leaned forward. "Let's take a look."

He reluctantly opened his mouth.

"Aha!" the dentist said. He poked at a tooth. "Does this hurt?"

"Aaargh!" Carlos screamed. "Yes, it does."

"Well, my friend," the dentist continued, "you have a cavity."

A cavity! "Does that mean you're going to pull my tooth out?" Carlos said with fear in his voice.

The dentist smiled. "No, it doesn't look like we'll have to pull it. We can just fix it, if that's OK with you."

Carlos smiled back. "You mean you're not going to use pliers?"

The dentist laughed in surprise. "Pliers? We don't use things like that."

Carlos realized then that the boy in the waiting

room hadn't been telling him the truth. The boy had just wanted to scare him. Carlos didn't think that was very nice at all. Not—at—all!

"OK," Carlos said, "you can fix my tooth. Are you going to do it now?"

"Yes, I am," the dentist said.

Then Carlos closed his eyes and said a silent prayer. He asked Jesus for strength and courage. After he finished praying, he opened his eyes and said, "OK, Doc! Go ahead."

And you know what? It wasn't that bad after all!

---

*I can do everything by the power of Christ.*
*He strengthens me.*
Philippians 4:13

# Roses for Natasha

*A Story about Coveting and Contentment*

Natasha was an artist. She loved to paint pictures of trees and flowers. Right now she was working on a special picture for a school contest. Natasha had been working on this picture for three weeks, and she wanted it to be perfect. She wanted to win first prize.

"Whatcha doing?" asked Stacy, Natasha's little sister.

"I'm working on my picture. Isn't it beautiful?" Natasha said as she dabbed a little more paint here and a little more paint there.

45

"Yeah!" Stacy said. "I wish I could paint like you. Can I help?"

"No! Why don't you leave me alone so I can concentrate?" Natasha said as she carefully chose another color.

Later that day, after dinner, Natasha, Stacy, and their mom and dad had family devotions. They sang a few songs, and then Mom read a verse from the Bible. Afterward, they discussed the verse, which was about coveting a neighbor's possessions.

"What does that mean, Mom?" Natasha asked, her eyebrows wrinkling.

"Well, coveting means that you want what belongs to your neighbor," Mom said.

"Oh," Natasha replied. But she really didn't understand what was so wrong with that.

The next day after school, Natasha stopped in front of Mr. Jacobs's house. Mr. Jacobs had a beautiful rose garden. "Wow! I wish I had some roses like that," Natasha said to herself. "I bet

Mom would really love to have some big, beautiful roses too."

Natasha wanted the roses so much, so she went and picked some. One, two, three, four, five beautiful yellow roses. She picked all the roses on the bush. There were so many other flowers in the yard that Natasha figured Mr. Jacobs wouldn't miss a few.

Natasha took the roses home and put them in a vase for Mom to see. After she had arranged the flowers nicely, she went to her room to work on her picture.

As she walked into the room, she let out a scream that echoed through the whole house. Someone had painted birds on her picture!

"Stacy!" Natasha yelled.

Stacy ran into the room. "What's the matter?" she asked.

"You painted on my picture," Natasha accused. "Look at it!"

Stacy paused for a moment, admiring the picture. "Isn't it beautiful? I wanted to paint like you.

So I tried to make it more beautiful by painting some birds."

Natasha was very angry. "I told you not to touch my picture. You ruined it for me," she said with tears in her eyes. "You ruined it!"

Natasha was so angry that she ran out of the house. She kept on running until she got to Mr. Jacobs's house. Mr. Jacobs was out in his yard, and he looked mad too. He was kicking the dirt with his boots and muttering to himself.

Natasha stopped running. "Mr. Jacobs, what's the matter?" she asked.

Mr. Jacobs looked up at her. "I've spent months and months working on my garden. And now it looks like someone just came and yanked out my special yellow roses. I was growing them for a flower show," he said.

Natasha felt awful. She had picked his special yellow roses! She hadn't thought he would notice if they were gone. After all, he had so many flowers in his yard.

"Mr. Jacobs," she said softly.

"What is it?" he asked.

"Mr. Jacobs," she said again, trying to be brave, "I'm the one who picked your flowers."

"You did what?" he said. He looked very angry.

"I thought they were very beautiful, and so I wanted them," Natasha said quickly. "I didn't think I was doing anything wrong. You have so many flowers."

Mr. Jacobs was quiet for a minute, then said, "Why didn't you ask me for some flowers instead of just taking them?"

"I don't know. I'm sorry," said Natasha. She felt so bad.

"Well, Natasha," Mr. Jacobs said, shaking his head, "I'm very disappointed in you, but I'll accept your apology."

Even though Mr. Jacobs had forgiven her, Natasha headed back home with a heavy heart. When she got there, she found Stacy sitting on the couch with tears in her eyes. Natasha walked over to Stacy and put her arms around her.

"Stacy, I know just how you feel," she said softly.

"You did a bad thing by wanting my painting. But I did a bad thing too. I wanted Mr. Jacobs's roses, and I took some. I can paint another picture, but I can't replace Mr. Jacobs's roses."

Just then, Mom came home. "Oh, my! Look at the roses," she said in a happy voice. Then she saw the sad looks on Natasha and Stacy's faces. "What's the matter with you two?"

"Mom, something terrible happened today," Natasha said sadly. "Those roses are from Mr. Jacobs's garden. I wanted them, so I took them without asking. Now I ruined his chances of getting a prize at the flower show."

"Yeah, Mom," added Stacy, "and I messed up Natasha's painting. I wanted to paint like her, and now her picture is ruined."

Mom gave both of the girls a hug. "Well, it sounds like you two learned a bit more about the word 'coveting,'" she said tenderly. "You see, God wants us to be content with what we have and not wish for what someone else has."

Natasha nodded her head. "I understand now, Mom. And I'll try very hard not to covet again."

"Me too!" Stacy said.

---

*Be happy with what you have.*
Hebrews 13:5

# Shortcuts

*A Story about Doing Your Best*

It was a beautiful summer morning at Camp Hale. The air was warm, the sky was blue, and the birds were singing in the gentle breeze. Carlos thought it was much too nice outside to be inside cleaning. He and his friend Danny, whom he shared a bunk bed with at camp, were assigned cleanup duty for the morning. They were supposed to clean the bunkhouse for inspection.

"Boy, if there's one thing I don't like, it's cleanup duty," Carlos said. "What a waste of time!"

"Yeah," Danny said, "but everyone has to do it. Each bunk has their day, and today is our day."

"Yeah, but I don't like it," Carlos complained. "Let's just get it over with."

They decided that the best way to get the job done was to split up the work. Carlos would do one side of the bunkhouse, while Danny did the other.

So Carlos began to sweep his side, while Danny swept his. Danny made sure each and every corner of his side was swept thoroughly. He liked to make sure a job was well done. But Carlos just swept the dirt underneath the beds. He liked to get things done as quickly as possible, even if that meant taking shortcuts.

Pretty soon, Carlos was on his way out the door.

"Hey, Carlos, where are you going? We aren't finished cleaning the bunkhouse."

"I'm finished," Carlos replied as the door slammed behind him.

When Danny finished cleaning his side of the bunkhouse, he went outside to find Carlos.

"Hey, Carlos," he said, "how did you clean up so fast?"

"Shortcuts, my friend," Carlos said with a smile. "Shortcuts."

Later that day, Mr. Jim, their camp counselor, gathered all the boys around. Mr. Jim was a tall, friendly man who always wore a big silver whistle around his neck. He blew on the whistle to quiet down the boys.

"All right, guys, pay attention," he said. "Today we're going to learn how to put up a tent."

Carlos didn't like the sound of that. *Who needs this? I know how to put up a tent,* he thought.

Mr. Jim continued talking. "When you put up your tent, make sure you have a good foundation." Then he talked about how to unroll the tent, how to place the pegs in the ground, and how to tie strong knots once the tent was up.

"Remember," Mr. Jim added, "tonight we'll be camping outside. I want to make sure you all understand how to put up your tents correctly with a good foundation. Are there any questions?"

Everyone had questions, except for Carlos. After the boys had everything figured out, they rolled up their tents, packed their lunches into their backpacks, and hiked to the campsite. Once they arrived there, they began putting up their tents.

"Hey, Carlos," Danny said, "do you need any help?"

"No. Putting up this tent is no big deal," Carlos said, waving his hand and smiling. "Shortcuts, my friend. There's always a shortcut." After all, a knot was a knot, and dirt was dirt. What harm could a couple of shortcuts cause?

As Carlos quickly put up his tent, Danny made sure every knot of his tent was tied tightly and every peg was placed firmly in the ground. Carlos finished putting up his tent before all of the other boys, then went down to the lake to skip stones across the water. When Danny was done, he went to the lake to join Carlos.

"I can't believe you finished so fast," Danny said. "How did you do it?"

Carlos just smiled at Danny.

"Oh, I know. Shortcuts, right?" Danny asked.

Carlos laughed and nodded his head. "That's right, buddy. Shortcuts."

Later that night, the boys gathered around the campfire and talked about the county fair near Camp Hale. In a few days, all the boys at camp would get to go to the fair. Carlos was very excited. He loved to go on rides and play games, much more than he liked cleaning bunkhouses and putting up tents.

Pretty soon it was time to go to bed. All of the boys climbed into their tents and quickly fell asleep. But during the night, rain began to fall from the sky. As the rain fell, the wind began to blow.

Carlos woke up. Something was dripping on his face. It was rain! He sat up and saw that he had left a flap of his tent open. But then he noticed something else. His tent was rocking back and forth in the strong wind, and it looked like it was about to fall on top of him!

Sure enough, that's exactly what happened. Down came the tent! Carlos wiggled his way out and into a giant mud puddle. He was very wet! He looked around at the other tents. They were all still standing. His was the only one that had fallen.

He ran over to Danny's tent. "Danny," he called, "can I come in?"

Danny unzipped his tent. "Carlos! You're all wet and muddy. What happened?"

"Let me in and I'll tell you. Hurry!"

Danny opened the tent flap, and Carlos crawled inside.

"My tent fell down," Carlos said as water dripped from his hair. "I got soaking wet crawling through the mud puddles. Can I sleep in your tent with you?"

"Sure," Danny said.

Carlos curled up at Danny's feet and shivered. He didn't have anything to cover himself with, since his sleeping bag was wet and still inside his fallen tent. Soon he began to sneeze.

The next day, Carlos didn't feel so good. Mr. Jim felt his forehead. It was hot. Carlos had a fever, so he had to stay in bed for a few days.

"What about the fair?" Carlos asked.

"Well, it looks like you can't go to the fair," Mr. Jim replied. "You're going to need plenty of rest so you can get better."

Carlos was quiet for a moment. "I wish I had put up my tent the right way," he finally said. "If I hadn't taken so many shortcuts, I would still be able to go to the fair."

"That's right," Mr. Jim said, giving Carlos a pat on the shoulder. "God wants us to do our best. We should never take the easy way out."

"That's for sure," Carlos said as he sneezed. "Because sometimes the easy way isn't so easy!"

---

*People who work hard are completely satisfied.*
Proverbs 13:4

# The Innocent Thief

*A Story about Thinking the Best*

"Heather, watch out!" Natasha yelled as a french fry flew past Heather's head.

"Yikes! That just missed me," Heather said as she frowned at the boys at the next table.

Lunch at Heather's school was always exciting. Today, the cafeteria had hamburgers and french fries for lunch, and the boys were having fun throwing fries at the girls.

"I wish those boys would be nice," Heather said. "They're always so naughty and noisy." She looked over to a table where a boy sat alone. "All the boys are noisy except for Brian. He always sits by himself."

"Yeah," Natasha agreed. "All the other boys think he's weird. He doesn't have many friends."

A little while later, the school bell rang. Lunchtime was over. Heather began cleaning up her lunch tray and picking up her books for class. As she picked up her notebook, she noticed something was missing. Her gold-colored pen was gone!

"Have you seen my gold pen?" Heather asked Natasha.

"No, I haven't seen it," Natasha replied as she ducked another french fry soaring through the air.

*Where could it be?* Heather thought. She got down underneath the table and looked on the floor. There were plenty of french fries and spilled milk down there, but no pen.

"I had it earlier today, but now I can't find it. Where could it be?" she mumbled.

When she got up from underneath the table, Natasha walked up to her.

"Heather," Natasha whispered, "I just threw away the trash on my lunch tray and walked past Brian's table. I saw your pen next to his notebook. I betcha he stole it."

Heather looked over at Brian. "Yeah, you're right, Natasha," she whispered back. "Brian probably did steal my pen. He's a thief."

"What did you say?" a boy at the next table asked. "Who's a thief?"

"Brian is," Natasha said. "He took Heather's gold pen."

The boy nodded his head. "I knew there was something weird about him." Then he told the other boys at his table about Brian. Pretty soon the whole cafeteria knew about Brian and Heather's gold pen.

Later that day, during class, the kids passed a folded piece of paper around the room. It said: "Brian is a thief!" Finally, the piece of paper landed on Brian's desk. He unfolded the paper, read it, then crumpled it in his hand. His face turned bright red, and he looked like he was going to cry.

One of the boys sitting right behind Brian leaned over his desk and whispered, "You're a thief, Brian. A plain ol' thief!"

Brian threw the wrinkled piece of paper on the floor. "I am not a thief!" he yelled.

The teacher, who was writing on the blackboard, quickly turned around. "What on earth is going on?" she demanded.

"Brian's a thief," Natasha blurted out. "He stole Heather's pen."

The teacher looked at Brian. "Is this true?" she asked.

Brian didn't answer. He just stared at the floor, tears forming in his eyes.

The teacher looked at Heather. "What do you have to say, Heather?" she asked.

"Well, I had a pen, but now it's missing," Heather replied. "Brian has my gold pen."

"Yeah," agreed one of the boys in the class. "Brian's a thief!"

"That's enough," the teacher said sternly as she walked to Brian's desk. She put her arm around Brian's shoulder.

"Brian, could you please show us your pen?" she asked softly. Brian looked at her face, then slowly reached into his desk and pulled out a shiny gold pen. The teacher took the pen and held it up for the class to see. "Is this the pen?"

"That's it!" Heather said. "That's my pen."

The teacher walked over to Heather. "Did you take a close look at this pen?" she asked.

"No, not . . . not really," Heather replied.

"I didn't think so," the teacher continued. "This is the pen I gave Brian earlier today. It has his initials on it: B. T., for Brian Thomas. It was his reward for having the highest grades for the last three months. Heather, I gave you a similar pen last fall when your grades were the highest, but this time it was Brian's turn. See, you just saw this gold pen and thought it was yours."

Heather's face turned red. She was very embarrassed.

"Why didn't you ask Brian about the pen before you accused him?" the teacher asked her.

"Well, Natasha told me he stole it," Heather replied in a shaky voice.

Now Natasha's face turned red. "Well . . . well . . . well, it looked like her pen to me," she said.

"I think you all owe Brian an apology," the teacher said to the whole class, "because he didn't steal anyone's pen. You all jumped to a false conclusion. We should make sure never to do that. God wants us to think the best of people, not to judge them."

Now everyone's faces turned red!

"All right, class, I think we've all learned a good lesson today. But now it's time to get back to the math lesson."

As the teacher turned to the board, a voice rang out in the air.

"Hey, here's my pen! It was in my desk all

along!" Heather yelled as a stale french fry sailed in her direction.

---

*To show mercy is better than to judge.*
James 2:13

# Never Enough

*A Story about Thankfulness*

"Hey, Natasha, let's go in here!" Karen tugged on Natasha's sleeve and guided her into a jewelry store. Karen was glad Natasha's mom had taken them to the shopping mall. Karen loved to shop and buy new things.

Once they were inside the store, Karen found something that she wanted very much. "Look at this necklace," she said to Natasha. "I've got to buy it!"

Natasha looked at the necklace. "It's very pretty. How much does it cost?"

Karen looked at the price tag. "Oh no," she said. "It costs ten dollars. I only have five."

"I guess you can't get it then," Natasha said.

"It's just not fair," Karen complained. "I never have enough money to buy what I want." She looked at Natasha. "What are you going to get?"

Natasha headed over to the hair clips. "Well, I was thinking about getting some of these barrettes."

"I wish I could get some barrettes too, but I don't have enough money," Karen whined. "I never have enough money."

"Yes, you do," Natasha said. "You always seem to have the latest things. You have nice clothes and toys."

"Come on, Natasha," said Karen. "You know what I mean."

"No, I don't."

"Oh well, nobody knows what I mean," Karen sighed. "How much money do you have, anyway?"

"I've got fifteen dollars."

"See what I mean?" Karen said. "You have more money than I do."

"But I've been saving it. Besides, you had ten dollars yesterday, didn't you?"

"Yeah," Karen said, "but I spent five dollars on baseball cards and candy."

Natasha picked out the barrettes that she wanted, then turned to Karen. "Well, are you going to get something, even if you can't get the necklace?"

Karen pouted. "If I can't get what I want, then I'm not going to get anything. I'm sick of shopping, anyway. I want to go home."

"OK, let me pay for this and we'll go," Natasha said.

When Karen got home, she found her mom and dad in the living room. "Mom, Dad, listen," she said. "I need a bigger allowance. I can't get all the things I want with what you're giving me."

Dad looked up from the newspaper. "Well, Karen, it was nice of you to say hello," he said jokingly. Then he became serious. "You're going to have to be satisfied with what you've got, because that's all I can afford to give you."

"Yes, Karen, you know money doesn't grow on trees," Mom added. "Your dad is already working two jobs in order to give you nice things."

"But everyone has nicer things than I have, and more money to spend. It's just not fair!" she yelled as she stomped out of the room.

She then ran up to her bedroom and slammed the door. "Why did I have to be born into this family?" she complained to herself. "Everyone else has nicer clothes and more things than I do."

Karen was so angry that she decided to stay in her room for the rest of the day. She didn't even say good-bye to her dad when he went to work at his nighttime job.

The next morning when she got up, Karen was surprised to see her grandma in the kitchen, making breakfast.

"Why are you here, Grandma?" Karen asked. "Where's Mom?"

Grandma turned around and smiled at Karen. "Come here, dear. Grandma needs to tell you something." She sat down on a chair and pulled Karen onto her lap.

Karen felt scared. "What's going on?"

"Well, dear," Grandma said, "Your mom had to go to the hospital."

"Why? What's the matter?"

Grandma hugged Karen close. "Your dad got sick last night when he was at work. He had to go to the hospital so the doctors could see what was wrong. And the doctors said that your dad had a heart attack."

A heart attack? That sounded bad. "Will Dad get better?" Karen asked, trying not to cry.

"Well, your mom went to see him in the hospital. That's why I'm here—to take care of you. She just called me and said that your dad is getting better. The doctors think he'll be all right."

Karen was so happy! She gave Grandma a big hug. Then she stopped. "But why did Dad have a heart attack?"

"The doctors think your dad has been working too hard. Sometimes having two jobs can be very difficult. Your dad will probably only be able to work at one job from now on."

Suddenly, Karen wasn't so happy anymore. She felt very bad. She knew Dad worked two jobs so that she could have nice things. And she had never been thankful for all the hard work Dad did. She had only thought about herself.

Grandma stayed with Karen for a few more days. Then Karen got to go with Mom to visit Dad in the hospital. Karen was very excited to see Dad. She had a few things she wanted to say to him.

When Karen got to Dad's hospital room, she ran in and gave him a big hug.

"How are you feeling?" she asked.

"I'm feeling much better," he replied.

Karen was quiet for a minute. "Dad," she finally said, "I have something I need to tell you."

"What's that, Karen?"

"I'm really sorry I yelled at you the other day. I'm sorry I wasn't thankful for all the nice things you give me. But I don't want to have so many nice things if it means you'll get sick again."

Dad smiled at her. "I accept your apology. And I'm going to try real hard not to get sick again. But that means I won't be able to work two jobs anymore. That also means you won't be able to have as many new things."

"That's OK, Dad," Karen said, giving him another hug. "I don't mind."

"Good. And I'm glad that you learned the importance of being thankful for the things that you have. It's very important to thank other people for the things they do for us, but it's even more important to give thanks to God for the things he does for us. And you know what I'm thankful to God for?"

"What?" Karen asked.

Dad smiled. "I'm thankful that God gave me a nice daughter like you!"

---

*Give thanks to the Lord.*
1 Chronicles 16:8

# About the Author

Hey, guys! My father asked me to write this since he is too shy to do it himself . . .

Joel Thompson is the author of the ClubZone Kids book series. At his youthful age (he asked me to put that in), he is also the creator of the *CMJ ClubZone* TV show from SonBurst Media and helped create the *BloodHounds, Inc.* TV series. He's starred in many New York Broadway shows, written and produced national TV commercials (my favorite was for Arby's), appeared on *The Tonight Show* and some show called *The*

*Merv Griffin Show,* written songs for grown-ups like Perry Como and Nell Carter, was a television producer and began at the famous award-winning Public Television hub WGBH Studios in Boston, and was a member of the New Christy Minstrels (whoever they are).

He graduated with honors from Charles E. Mackey Elementary School in Boston, where he was voted class clown four years running and elected President of the Hall Monitors of America Association. He was an excellent newspaper boy, and still found time to sell his used comic books to neighborhood kids.

Best of all, my dad—oops! ahem—Joel is also an ordained minister who speaks to churches and at conferences. He's not at all ready to settle down to one job. He wants to do and create too many things before he really grows up!

His all-time favorite food is "anything with cheese," and the real loves of his life are God, his wife, Vicki, and family, our cocker spaniel, Coco, and, of course, ME!

Heather Marie Thompson

# About CMJ ClubZone

More than 2.4 million fans tune in weekly to *CMJ (Come Meet Jesus) ClubZone* from SonBurst Media, a 30-minute national children's television program that reinforces faith, positive values, and self-esteem through a relationship with Jesus.

The show features Artie's Treehouse, the Curious Cam Man (portrayed by Joel Thompson), who investigates kids' questions with his video camera, and the ClubZone Kids, a diverse cast of talented youths who

- learn amazing facts about nature and archaeology
- sing lovable, positive songs
- discuss faith and values, and

- meet special guests like neurosurgeon and best-selling author Ben Carson *(Gifted Hands)*, star athletes from the Detroit Lions and the Green Bay Packers, plus doctors, judges, artists, educators and ministers from across America who share valuable insights from diverse professions in kid-friendly language.

Each of the season's 26 shows focus on a specific theme discussed by real kids. Music, laughter, drama, suspense, and Scripture follow, drawing young viewers closer to Jesus.

More than 10 additional independent networks around the globe carry the show, including The Inspirational Network, TCT, World Harvest Television, Total Living, Cornerstone TV, Dominion Sky Angel, Angel 1, Kids and Teens TV, MBC, and Australian Christian—reaching more than 42 million TV homes per week, and in some cases daily.

For more information about the TV series, videos, the *Kids Are Christians Too!* radio program and other extensions of the CMJ ClubZone interfaith, nonprofit ministry, write to . . .

CMJ ClubZone
P.O. Box 400
Niles, MI  49120

www.cmjclubzone.com

# Follow the

## CLUBZONE KIDS

## Through All Their Adventures...